Aspen Grove
Collection Of Poems

Alexey Soshalskiy

AlexeyPoetry

Contents

Aspen Grove

Music

There's always music playing,
Just take another glance;
The aspen trees are swaying,
And leaves begin to dance.

In spring the robins sing,
While sparrows learn to fly.
In fall the chimes will ring,
And leaves will rustle by.

And winter is a treat;
You'll hear the blizzards blow,
The sound of stepping feet
Upon the morning snow.

And when the summer starts
A charming song will blare;
The sound of beating hearts
When love is in the air.

So open up your soul,
You'll hear an angel praying.
The world is bright and whole;
There's always music playing...

April 24th, 2022.

Starry Dust

Tonight a chilling gust
Has left a frosty bedding,
Or maybe starry dust
The milky way is shedding?

The stars above are sprinkling
A hint of sugar glaze,
Now every roof is twinkling
Into a crystal haze.

My town is deep in sleep,
But when will come the day
The birches then will sweep
The starry dust away...

April 30th, 2022.

Beloved City

My dear beloved city,
For you I'll write a ditty.
Your features sing a song,
With them I'll sing along.

I'm charmed by all your looks;
Your warm and long chinooks.
Your winter and your spring,
Your birds that love to sing!

Your cozy starter homes,
Your jolly garden gnomes.
Your sprinklers and your hoses,
Your gardens filled with roses!

Your meek, yet raving breeze,
Your purple maple trees.
Your mighty blessed churches,
Your perfect silver birches.

Your river's tuneful streams,
That spark our youthful dreams.
Your sun, your warmth, your graces,
And all your friendly faces.

My dear beloved city,
For you I write this ditty.
To you I'll always cling,
For you I'll always sing.

March 20th, 2021.

Melting Snow

Oh snow, you fear me none!
You have no power here!
The time already won,
You'll have to wait a year!

Outside is blooming May!
You came a little late...
For soon you'll melt away,
Excuse me while I wait.

For spring will melt your cool,
Your frost will lose its powers,
And soon you'll be a pool
That feeds the blooming flowers!

And they will glow and grow,
I'll dance and mud my boots;
Because the woeful snow
Just cannot flood their roots!

Oh snow, you fear me none!
You have no power here!
We have the cheery sun,
To melt away the fear!

May 26th, 2021.

What A Day!

What a morning! What a day!
Birds awake and sing: "hurray!"
They peck and sing into my room,
They're telling me it's time to bloom!

I open up my windows wide,
I smell the air of spring outside,
"Hello! Hello my little starling!
Yes, you're right I'll kiss my darling!

Yes, you're right I'll change my habits!
I won't chase away the rabbits.
I'll even make some honest truces;
I won't fight the angry gooses...

I'll even get a crow to smile!
I'll even walk an extra mile!"
What a day and what a morning!
Not a cloud upstairs is storming!

Not a single head is butting,
Every berry bush is budding!
The cherries shine their rosy hue,
I might just pick a thing or two.

What a lovely, lovely day,
Even bunnies sing: "hurray!"
And so, I praise the bunny merits!
Even though they steal my carrots...

The bunnies wave the sun goodbye,
And now the moon is shining high.
The moon begins to sing ahead:
"It's time to sleep, it's time for bed."

The stars are now my final treat,
The stars: they make my joy complete!
What a day, and what a night;
What a lovely, lovely sight...

May 27th, 2021.

Ladybug

Thoughts of spring and thoughts of you
Bloomed this morning once anew!
I ponder in a hammock snug:
"Where's my dearest ladybug?"
I want to see her scarlet hues,
That bring to me exciting clues;
That spring at last has come to me,
To bloom again the apple tree!
My lady bug again is late,
My lady bug will tell me straight;
She'll tell me that I'm not alone,
That my dear is coming home.
My dear, you'd be so happy here,
I dream and wish you could appear.
So amidst a charming swoon
I'll again be loving June.
So amidst the skies of blue
I'll again be loving you.
Because I long the snows dismissal,
And dear I hold a sparrow's whistle.
And when I'll hear that sparrow yonder,
Then again, again I'll ponder

Thoughts of spring and thoughts of you.
Now upon a blooming view,
While laying in a hammock snug,
Flies to me my lady bug.

May 2nd, 2021.

Lotus

The willow tree is sappy,
A lotus swims alone.
My girlfriend is unhappy,
The reason is unknown...

Oh look! The frogs are hopping!
You see that duckling swim?
But yet your smile is dropping,
And now the sun is dim...

But since it's warm in June,
I'm sure your smile will leap!
Just like the rising moon
That puts the frogs to sleep.

My dear, you see that lotus,
That never seems to settle?
She wants for us to notice
Her rosy colour petal.

She wants to hear she's pretty,
But that she'll never mention.
She isn't seeking pity;
She only wants attention.

She wants to gleam and glow
The way you do, my dear...
And now I think I know
The words you want to hear.

So hear my poem and tune!
There's something I must say:
You're beautiful as June!
More beautiful than May...

June 4th, 2021.

Daffodil

The Daffodil has grown
Within a sunny day.
Its colours just have shone,
And now it wilts away....

The flower starts to fall,
The petals did not last.
And now our hearts recall
Of all the ones who passed.

They passed their living hour,
And now they're left unsung.
Like you, my little flower,
They leave us way too young...

They just have met a love,
They just have breathed the air;
They gazed the clouds above,
And now they're all up there.

It's hard to comprehend,
It pains the beating heart;
So many meet their end,
While some don't get to start...

May 6th, 2021.

Mighty River

I see a river flowing
In such a fleeting pace;
I'm asking where its going,
And why the sudden race?

And why must it devour
Everything in sight?
Where is my lily flower
That was shining light?

River, mighty river!
You swept it all away...
Please may you deliver
My lily back today.

Or maybe you'll just hint
To where my flower swam?
I'm praying that it didn't
Approach a beaver dam.

And as the river's flowing
It splits my heart in two;
I'm asking where it's going,
And may it take me too!

May 4th, 2021

The Bunny

The sky again is sunny,
The garden gate is squeaking;
And there I see a bunny
Just underneath it peeking.

Oh bunny, you're my fellow,
This girl, I wish you knew her;
She lights the lilies yellow,
And now the sky is bluer!

I tell the mini hare
About my heart and mood,
He doesn't really care,
He only wants some food...

But I am not pretending,
This girl is in my head;
Her beauty finds no ending,
She turns the roses red!

She turns the willows greener,
My heart just cannot bare it!
If bunny just have seen her
He would forget the carrot...

And now the skies are sunny!
And now I care again!
All right, my little bunny,
Have a carrot then!

July 1st, 2021.

To Mother

Oh Mother, dearest Mother,
Your love has helped me greatly.
I just have heard from brother
That you've been tired lately.

And that you've hurt your back,
From everything it carries.
Oh Mother, I'll be back,
I'll pick the garden berries.

I'll lift the water can,
I'll feed the garden whole.
I'll do the best I can,
I'll dig whatever hole.

There's much you carried here;
You raised a hooligan.
I promise you won't hear
The calls from school again.

You taught me much before
When I was just a child,
And now you'll teach me lore
On how to plant the wild.

I'll plant a daffodil,
For us to see and boast.
Because in Staffordville;
We'll see it shine the most.

And it will cheer the town,
And it will love us greatly.
Oh Mother, please sit down,
Cause you've been tired lately.

June 17th, 2021.

Dandelion

My dandelion, you grow
In such a lively speed;
And though with love you glow,
We label you a weed...

We label you a pain,
The way we do with others.
Now isn't it insane
Of how a neighbour smothers?

And how a neighbour kills,
And how he loves to scold;
How much of Staffordsville's
Dandelions get pulled.

We disregard so many
Like they're pollution waste,
And of the people, plenty
Can never be replaced.

Oh dandelion, my dear,
To me you don't pollute.
And don't be filled with fear,
I'll never pull your root.

May 8th, 2021.

Traits

I hate to fight and diss,
I'd rather hug and kiss.
The flaws my spirit hates
Have now become my traits...

I'm up and then I'm down,
I smile and then I frown.
I'm mad that I am sad,
And sad that I am mad.

I hate that I will fight
So I can prove I'm right;
I want to be so meek
That I can turn a cheek.

I want to be so humble
That pride itself can crumble!
One day you'll find me strange
Because I'll truly change.

And like the linden trees
My heart will bloom with ease!
I will not fight and diss,
But rather hug and kiss!

October 21st, 2021.

Starry Night

Many nights I spend alone,
So to the stars I sneak.
Is there someone for me to phone?
Someone with whom to speak?

Stars, you warm my heart with shiver,
In the dark you're bright.
Tiny specks of sterling silver
Swimming in the night.

May 29th, 2021.

The One

I'll find my one, one day,
And darling, you will too.
We're in the month of May,
Our flowers barely grew.

I'd hate to be the jerk,
I'd hate to see you crying.
Together we wont work,
So what's the point of trying?

You'll find your one, one day,
I promise you it's true.
You're in the month of May,
Your flowers barely grew.

Someone else will raise
Your heart into the sky.
To the lonely days
You soon will say goodbye.

You'll say goodbye to May,
And then "the one" will show,
And on that perfect day
You'll see your flowers grow.

July 24th, 2021.

With Colour Shines My Yard

With colour shines my yard,
The sunshine moves a pen.
The times are always hard
Before they're good again.

The smoke is almost gone,
There is no doom impending;
And in a book I've drawn
A sweet and joyful ending.

I'm still a little weak,
But now the air is lighter.
I heard the willow speak:
"The future will be brighter."

Anxieties will loom,
The waves will come and go,
And peonies will bloom
From underneath the snow.

There's still some smoky air,
But now I feel it thinning;
And through the sunny glare
I'll draw a new beginning!

Where colour shines my yard,
Where sunshine moves a pen,
Where times are never hard,
Where times are good again...

August 7th, 2021.

Nightingale

Oh Nightingale, your songs
Complete the rest of May!
And now the summer longs
A girl that's far away.

Your songs are such a treat,
And no more frosty pelts.
With every chirp and tweet
Another snowflake melts.

Now fly, my nightingale
Where flowers wilt and curl!
And in a snowy vale
Is where you'll meet a girl.

Tell her that a boy
Is wishing her the best.
Sing her songs of joy,
And make yourself a guest.

So you can show her heart
A garden shining spring!
And rivers flowing art
With every song you sing.

And if she's cold you seem,
Then sing away the snow;
So daisies glow with gleam,
So lilies gleam with glow!

And if she's with another,
Don't tweet it back to me;
Oh please, don't even bother,
If so, then let it be...

May 29th, 2021.

Silver Cross

At nights I turn and toss,
I feel the birches breeze.
A sterling silver cross
Is what my village sees.

The sterling silver shines
Across my Staffordville,
And all the power lines
Are shaking by the thrill.

The ville is my abode,
It's here I also search
To find a straighter road,
Is it the Slavic church?

The weeping birches wave
Towards the shining light;
They're saying it will save
The world from utter night.

At nights I turn and toss,
I yearn to find my glee.
Oh Sterling Silver Cross,
Are you calling me?

July 12th, 2021.

Renewal

The freezing winter storm
Has met the summer heat;
The garden now is warm,
The raspberries are sweet.

My dear, I was judgemental,
But now I'm so forgiving!
I've grown to be so gentle,
I've grown to be so giving.

Today I argue little,
I do not yell and bug.
I now would not belittle
The smallest ladybug.

My heart has seen reform!
And if by chance we meet,
My hug would be so warm,
My kiss would be so sweet...

If fate was rearranged,
I'd hope that you could see
How much I've really changed,
How gentle I can be...

My freezing winter storm
Has met the summer heat;
The garden now is warm,
The raspberries are sweet.

July 25th, 2021.

Finish Line

With every storm, with every night,
There is a glimpse of shining light.
With every race, with every pain
There is a grace that we attain.

Do good, be good, and never sway,
And head towards the righteous way.
And when you reach the finish line
I promise you it will be fine.

October 20th, 2021.

To Father

Behold the man who held the world
At times that atlas could not hold.
And with the strength of heart and soul
He kept our planet safe and whole.

He held the world with mighty shoulders,
He moved the clouds and mountain boulders;
He built a gorgeous blessed church
Where mighty angels made their perch.

He gazed into the trail of doubt,
But yet he always found a route.
A cross is shining over him,
A light that never seems to dim.

He sang with light, he sang through night,
He kept a smile with every fight.
And when he sings with exclamation
The cosmos shakes with fascination!

The wicked fall towards the ground,
The righteous raise towards the sound!
And every country, every race
Will hear the voice of Slavic base!

A voice so dear, a voice so kind,
A voice that's truly hard to find.
The man is great, he's like no other,
This man I love, he is my father.

November 7th, 2021.

Alberta

Alberta, beloved dear,
Your beauty isn't wrong;
I always love to hear
Your humble prairie song.

Your aspen trees have bowed
To skies of singing geese.
When life is way too loud
Somehow you bring me peace.

Your twinkle shining creeks
That run through haven farms,
Your rocky mountain peaks
That reach to Heaven's arms.

With grace empowered hands
They laid a golden bedding.
My daisy flowered lands,
Where is your spirit heading?

One day we'll reach the stairs;
Your sky is blue and clear.
I'm thankful in my prayers
That God has placed me here.

Alberta, I'm sorry dear,
Your beauty isn't wrong,
Not everyone can hear
Your humble prairie song.

November 17th, 2021.

Unforgiving Fall

The sun is uninspired
To sing a merry song;
The days are growing tired,
The nights are getting long.

Oh fall, you're unforgiving,
Your frost is drawing nigh,
The roses that were living
Today have said goodbye...

And in this cold ravine
My heart is also numbing,
Right now the leaves are green,
They don't know what is coming.

As I myself don't know
Of what will be of me;
I don't know where to go,
My path is hard to see.

Perhaps a friend will trick me,
A girl will tear my heart.
The summers end so quickly,
And yet they never start.

The robins hear their call,
And now they fly away.
My unforgiving fall,
Oh can you please delay?

August 26th, 2021.

23

The years are flying swift,
Today I'm twenty-three;
I just received a gift:
The brightest linden tree!

Oh linden tree, let's set
Our feet through years to come!
And may we both forget
Of where our roots are from.

And may we move along
Through all the thin and thick.
Let's wish our joy is long,
And hope the grief is quick...

Oh linden tree I ask:
"What life to us will bring?"
In autumn we will bask
The flowers of the spring!

For life is just a gift,
Like you, my linden tree.
And years are running swift,
Today I'm twenty-three...

October 24th, 2021.

Geese

The geese are flying high,
They're headed for the west.
Eternal azure sky,
You're weighing on my chest.

I've never understood
Why others like to flee.
To people I was good,
And they've forgotten me.

The ones I held so dear
Have slapped away my hands.
Perhaps it's cold in here,
They search for warmer lands...

Above the prairie grass
The geese disown the east.
The memories that pass
I do not miss the least...

May 1st, 2022.

Maple Leaf

I am a fallen maple leaf,
My summer joy was only brief.

An unexpected autumn day
Has made me wilt and fall away.

Or maybe someone had me hewn?
Or maybe winter came too soon?

And now from far below I'll sing,
And watch how other leaves will spring.

I left my home, I left my tree,
There is no turning back for me.

Another couple songs I'll make
Before I see the garden rake.

So sing, my green and leafy friends!
Before your summer quickly ends...

Aspen Grove

I am a fallen maple leaf,
My youthful joy was only brief.

December 12th, 2021.

Snow In Staffordville

Again the cotton snow
Has set on Staffordville.
And now the coulees glow,
The rivers start to chill...

The chickadees are hiding,
They've gone into their beds;
The little kids are riding
Their toboggans and sleds.

The village cat is rolling
Within a snowy puddle.
A lonely dog is strolling,
He wants someone to cuddle.

And still some leaves will glint
From underneath the snow;
This is the final hint
Of summer months ago.

A silver frost is sweeping
The day into the night;
My Staffordville is sleeping
Beneath a world of white.

A snowy queen is singing
Throughout the snowy drifts.
A bearded man is bringing
To us some warming gifts!

The snow is coming down,
The night is standing still
Within my charming town,
Within my Staffordville!

October 29th, 2021.

Winter Birches

Oh winter, tell me, please,
What will the future bring?
The frozen linden trees
Are yearning for the spring.

I'm like the linden tree
That waits to bloom and grow,
But yet I love to see
The birches in the snow.

Oh winter, free the pines,
Oh winter, bring me light;
Your canvas faintly shines
With colours black and white.

Your beautiful in all
Your sadness and your glory.
Your joy is quick and small
Like a romantic story.

It's like the world expired
Beneath a snowy pile.
The sky is even tired,
It doesn't show a smile...

And nothing seems to be,
And nothing seems to grow,
But still I love to see
The birches in the snow.

December 9th, 2021.

Christmas Carols

The Christmas carols play
Across my Staffordville,
The children ride their sleigh
Upon a snowy hill.

The Christmas snow is gold,
So may the blizzard swarm!
And though my feet are cold,
I feel my chest is warm.

The gifts that Santa brings
My youthful heart adores.
And Frank Sinatra sings
In all the nearby stores.

The churches sang and blessed
My little charming town,
The birches now are dressed
Into their winter gown.

The Christmas carols play,
Our houses we adorn;
For on this very day
Our Life and Joy was Born!

December 14th, 2021.

Silver Moon

The stars above are blushing,
They love the lunar crescent.
The men below are rushing
To buy their love a present.

I too have bought a gift
To give to someone dear;
Within the Christmas drift
I wish to bring some cheer.

Oh moon, oh silver moon,
This gift, why did I buy it?
Perhaps it's way too soon,
Perhaps the heart is quiet.

The silver moon replies:
"Get ready for a ride!
Within the glowing skies,
A star will be your guide.

Your darling does exist,
Your path will spin and twirl!
Behind a starry mist
You'll find a singing girl.

You'll think that you have slept,
You'll see amazing lands.
The gift that you have kept,
Will fall into her hands."

December 21st, 2021.

New Year's Eve

Oh New Year's, New Year's Eve!
Another era ends.
So many people leave,
I guess they weren't my friends...

Perhaps my reputation
Has caused some kind of scandal.
Perhaps my exclamation
Was much for them to handle.

A path begins to glow!
A road begins to bend.
This year I got to know
Who truly is my friend.

December 31st, 2021.

The Judge

Oh humans, we should mourn!
We're all so much alike;
A father we will scorn,
A brother we will strike.

Oh heart, I hear you beat,
But can you be more mute?
Why did we have to eat
The cursed forbidden fruit?

The sin could make me sink,
And burn me into vapor;
It is the blackest ink
That stains the whitest paper.

Or maybe darkness built me
From the corrupted ground.
I know, I know I'm guilty,
I wish to turn around.

I wish to see my Father,
Although my heart is foreign;
For one way or another
We all will stand before Him...

Oh clouds, will you relent?
And do you hold a grudge?
My Lord, I do repent!
You are my righteous judge.

December 26th, 2021.

The Master

Such shame it's almost funny
On what you made your goal;
You cling to so much money,
You cling with all your soul...

You thought that you were free?
You're just another slave.
Like me, you too will be
A name upon a grave.

And so you then commend
That money has a worth;
I promise you my friend,
It will not leave the earth.

The thought to you is deadly
Because your end is starting.
I ask would you have fed me
If you have found me starving?

Such shame it's almost funny,
And what a sad disaster;
You thought you mastered money,
When money was your master...

July 16th, 2021.

Mother's Garden

Across these maple lands
The linden trees were growing,
And in my mother's hands
The strawberries were glowing.

My thoughts... I cannot guard them
From anxious adversaries.
I miss my mother's garden,
The apples and the berries.

I'm not a loyal member
Towards the winter way.
As soon as it's December,
My heart falls back to May.

When apple colour dyes
Was all that I could see.
When linden flower skies
Were shining down on me.

The linden trees were growing
Across these maple lands.
The strawberries were glowing
Within my mother's hands.

My mother then would say:
"Here Alex, have a treat."
Those days were back in May,
Those days were truly sweet.

December 28th, 2021.

The Guest

The stars are glowing white,
The stars are deep in rest.
Upon this lonely night
A weight is on my chest.

Within my neighbourhood
My friends have gone astray,
Just like my childhood
That slowly fades away...

Is there a door to knock?
Someone to pour a drink?
Upon my roof I walk,
And in the stars I sink.

The stars are glowing white,
The stars are deep in rest;
If I could make the flight
Would they accept a guest?

April 23th, 2022.

Scarlet Rose

Oh rose, oh scarlet rose!
You come with heavy pricing...
The way your beauty glows
Is truly so enticing.

How many have you torn?
How many have you tricked?
And with your viscous thorn
How many have you pricked?

Oh rose, oh scarlet rose!
Your petals shine perfection.
My fate like river flows,
But not in your direction...

For if I were your lover,
My poetry won't bud.
And then my heart you'll cover
In rosy colour blood.

So may you cry and mourn,
Your stem I still won't pick.
And with your viscous thorn
A different heart you'll prick...

February 7th, 2022.

Ember Skies

I don't know what I'm seeing,
I don't believe my eyes;
It's like the world is fleeing
Beneath the ember skies.

Where is the future turning?
And who is there to blame?
The clouds above are burning,
And tears won't quench a flame...

We're not on Noah's ark,
But rather in a drought,
It takes a single spark,
For flames to burn us out...

May 14th, 2022.

The River

Oh river, tell me, please,
If I am flying straight.
Your bright reflection sees
What is my life and fate.

How quick your waves can run,
Makes everyone look slow;
And when you meet the sun
A million diamonds glow.

Oh river, tell me, please,
How come my spirit stings?
Across the prairie breeze
I fly with broken wings.

Perhaps your graceful motion
Will be my inspiration;
Perhaps the Heaven's Ocean
Will be our destination.

Oh river, may you flow it
Into the right direction,
Because a youthful poet
Is seen in your reflection...

April 7th, 2022.

Tomorrow

Today the skies are grey,
Tomorrow they'll be blue.
The snow won't always stay,
The sun will rise anew!

The sun will shine and graze
The land for many miles,
The daisy-coloured rays
Will bloom a million smiles.

Again the honey bees
Will form a honeycomb,
And with the aspen trees
I'll sing a sunny poem!

No longer will I shiver,
But rather dance instead.
Into a flowing river
I'll dunk my stupid head!

May water wash away
Anxieties that grew.
Today the skies are grey,
Tomorrow they'll be blue.

February 14th, 2022.

Early Spring

I love the early spring,
A gifted new beginning!
The robins spread their wing,
And soon they will be singing.

My anxious heart unfreezes,
And rivers start to flow,
Because the southern breezes
Have melted all the snow.

Within a prairie field
The bunnies leave their beds.
The dandelions revealed
Their little yellow heads.

The prairies light with gold,
The sky is glowing blue.
And everything of old
Is now becoming new!

The robins now are tweeting:
"We're gifted to restart!"
The earth is slowly heating,
Just like my youthful heart.

April 8th, 2022.

Rosy Skies

The sun is setting down,
The sunshine curtain closes;
Above my little town
The sky lights up with roses.

Above my little head
Another world appears,
The sky is blue and red,
Like fire mixed with tears.

My rosy colour sky,
You're beautiful to see,
But yet I'm asking why
You look so sad to me.

Perhaps an angel cries,
Or maybe I am yearning
To reach the highest skies
From where there's no returning.

My rosy colour skies,
I fear that I will stall;
The higher that I rise,
The harder is the fall...

March 17th, 2022.

Dangerous Route

I'll take the dangerous route,
And do not wish me luck.
The clouds will pull me out
If both my feet are stuck.

The world is in a night;
And so I wish to spark this.
To show the people light
I'll have to live in darkness.

They'll pierce my back with arrows,
They'll sucker me with blows.
Instead of charming sparrows,
I'll have to fly with crows.

And if my wings get stuck,
The clouds will set me free.
So do not wish me luck,
But rather pray for me...

April 1st, 2022.

Starling

The spring again is starting
Like everything is new!
Today I heard a starling;
It made me think of you.

For you the world is springing
Into a scarlet hue.
For you my heart is singing
The way the starlings do...

For you my garden shines
To all the neighbour porches;
Now all the grumpy pines
Have fell in love with birches!

The lilac scent arose,
And in the wind perfumes.
A lovely scarlet rose
Beneath your window blooms.

For spring again is starting!
And everything is new.
Today I heard a starling;
It made me think of you...

March 25th, 2022.

Elegy For Ukraine

The terror that I'm seeing
I pray it won't be long;
Cause every human being
Is like another song.

Some people are a flute,
They play a tune so sweet.
But yet some hearts are mute,
They do not make a beat...

Some people are the voice,
And to the clouds they pray.
We often don't rejoice
That we can breathe today...

Some hearts are like guitars
With warm and gentle strings.
And some have reached the stars,
With them an angel sings...

I do not have a clue
What instrument I play;
Into the Heavens blue
My song will fly someday.

For all these precious songs
One day will make a flight.
And all our rights and wrongs
Will be revealed in light.

The terror that I'm seeing
I pray it won't be long;
Cause every human being
Is like another song.

February 25th, 2022.

Love

Oh love, you are a trial,
For you I'm always trying;
You make my spirit smile,
But yet the heart is crying.

Some people like to give,
While others like to steal.
The more with love you live,
The more the pain you feel.

And maybe this is why
I tightly grasp my chest;
For only in the sky
A soul can truly rest.

For love is like the night,
And yet a sunny ray.
For love is black and white,
I've never seen it gray.

So may you all enjoy
The sunshine and the rain;
For love is friends with joy,
But relative to pain...

March 24th, 2022.

Troubled Son

Through every danger that I crossed
I always felt protection.
And every time that I was lost
I always found direction.

And when I lived the life I feared,
When everything would hurt,
Just like a dream you then appeared,
And picked me from the dirt.

And here I am, your troubled son,
I'm starting to relive this;
Repeating wrongs that I have done,
Then begging for forgiveness.

And over and over the same mistakes,
My lack of self control.
Oh Father, tell me what it takes
To heal my troubled soul.

Give me guidance and correction,
Give wings the strength to soar!
Give me meaning and direction
The way you did before...

March 20th, 2022.

Prairie Knoll

Across my swinging hair
The prairie wind is grazing;
A song begins to flare,
The music is amazing.

Upon the ledger lining
I feel symphonic notes,
The clouds above are shining
Like soft and fluffy coats!

I fall on to the grass,
Upon a prairie knoll;
A holy Latin Mass
Is playing in my soul.

June 7th, 2022.

Seasons

It's hard to move a pen
At times the soul is sore.
It's hard to love again
When you have loved before.

The heart becomes like rust,
That no one wants to touch.
It's hard to truly trust,
When you've been burned so much.

I don't know all the reasons
On why the world is strange.
Just like the passing seasons,
Our life will surely change.

My dear poetic friends,
We all have broken hearts!
Another season ends,
Another season starts...

January 14th, 2022.

Cyan Flower

Oh cyan flower sky,
Send blessings on our tomb.
Each one on earth will die,
But you will stay in bloom.

A temple I will build
To pray the holy scroll.
Ukrainian hymns have filled
The hollows of my soul.

I'll pray for those who wane,
That they may fly to you;
Oh Heaven, send your rain,
So I can flourish too.

Bestow your holy Mass,
Bestow your righteous hand!
We're in an hourglass,
We're falling like the sand...

And though on earth we die,
We ask for souls to bloom.
Oh cyan flower sky,
Send blessings on our tomb.

June 2nd, 2022.

Rainy May

I love it when it rains
Within the month of May!
The newly seeded grains
Are getting drunk today.

The winter mud is slushed,
It's flowing down the gutter.
The feelings that I hushed
I'll sing without a stutter!

Upon my roof and siding
A runnel starts to run.
I see a robin hiding,
He's waiting for the sun...

Oh robin, wait a few,
The mother clouds will ween;
The sky will flare with blue,
The grass will bloom with green!

I love it when it rains
Within the month of May.
It's like my deepest pains
Are being washed away...

May 20th, 2022.

Lovely Curse

Tonight the music plays,
In bed I turn and toss.
Outside a willow sways
Reflecting lunar gloss.

I cannot sleep tonight,
The music is too great...
A pen so small and light
Will push away the weight

Through silver stars I graze,
I'm catching music notes!
At first it's just a phrase,
And then some tuneful quotes.

And then a symphony
Is grandly orchestrated!
And yet it seems to me
There's nothing I've created...

I'm just a singing wren,
I'm just another writer;
And so I swing my pen
To make my shoulders lighter.

I have to write this verse
So I can sleep tonight;
It is my lovely curse,
My terrible delight...

June 7th, 2022.

The Painter

Oh painter, darling, please,
Your talent takes me high!
I love your aspen trees,
Your cherry colour sky.

Is it the skies creation
That turns the forest lush?
Or your imagination
That moves the paint and brush?

And now you filled my mind
With Heaven's earthly bliss.
A soul that's pure and kind
Can only paint like this...

For Heaven thought of earth
Without a single tainting.
I see my place of birth
Inside your lovely painting.

I cannot help but smirk,
I love you for your art;
Because your precious work
Has touched a poet's heart.

April 1st, 2022.

20 Years

Twenty years have passed
Since I have seen your face;
Into the overcast
You left without a trace.

There's barb upon your wires,
It will not let me breach.
Each one of us desires
The things we cannot reach...

But that's how life is drawn,
Our dear ones we ignore;
As soon as they are gone,
We start to love them more.

And now I sing with tears
Across a prairie glen.
Perhaps in twenty years
I'll see your face again.

April 4th, 2022.

White Aspens

Imagine: pains are put to ease,
And hearts are free of strains;
It's like a field of aspen trees
Without the darker stains.

And this is nothing but a hint,
Above is mighty better;
These sights are just a piece of lint
That fell from Father's sweater.

Recall when hearts are beating loud,
And songs are filled with mirth;
It's almost like the whitest cloud
Has landed on the earth.

The times we feel a warm connection,
With joyful smiles of love;
These moments are a slight reflection
Of Heaven from above.

May 30th, 2022.

Prairie Wind

The prairie wind is blowing,
And spring again is springing!
The dandelions are growing
With every petal swinging.

The dazzling trees of lind
Are slowly beautifying;
And soon the prairie wind
Will send the cotton flying!

I also wish to be
A cotton floating pearl,
So I can shine and flee
Towards my favourite girl.

So may the prairie wind blow!
I'll fly towards my dear!
I'll knock upon her window
To tell her spring is here...

May 11th, 2022.

Yesterday's Rain

Just yesterday it rained,
The grass is getting greener;
It's like my sins are drained,
And now the soul is cleaner.

For Heaven birds are singing!
For miracles they search!
The copper bells are ringing
Above a wooden church.

And green becomes the moss,
With life the trees are fed!
Towards the silver cross
I'm bowing down my head.

There's nothing else to do,
I'm praying as I wait.
Oh holy Heavens blue,
I ask to bloom my fate.

May 21, 2022.

Aspen Grove

My dearest aspen grove,
You are my favourite view!
For half a year I strove
To be again with you.

I'm glad that you survived
The freezing winter weather;
And now that I arrived,
We'll sing a song together!

Oh aspen grove, you know
That summer soon will be!
But yet you look like snow
On every single tree...

I love your snowy bark,
It shines a marble white;
Within a world so dark
I wish to live with light.

My dearest aspen grove,
You are my favourite view!
And many miles I drove
To be again with you.

April 27th, 2022.

Alphabetical List of Titles

About the Author

My name is Alexey Soshalskiy, and I am from Alberta, Canada. I am very new to poetry, I put together my first poem at the age of 22. I cannot exactly say what made me want to write poetry, however, I can say who have helped me learn how to write classic poems. I can thank my mother for teaching me the importance of rhythm, and the art of using stressors of words to create a melodious tune. I would also like to thank my father, Philology Dr. Andy Soshalskiy for teaching me the structure and art of writing short, but meaningful poems; as well as proofreading my first entire collection of poems: Aspen Grove.

AlexeyPoetry

33022200R00068